Welcome to the world of the Tree Ninjas!

Are they good at their job? Sometimes...
Are they clever? Thats debatable...
Do they have the necessary skills to make this book more interesting? Oh yes they do!

Join Ben, Jack, Martina, and whole group of hard working equipment on their journey through everyday life in the world of tree surgery.

The stories told in this book are based loosely on a real tree surgery company run by a man called Ben (me).
I have had the amazing pleasure of working with some brilliant characters over the years, which are brought to life inside.

Will it make you become a tree surgeon? Probably not.
Will it make you laugh? ummm, 1000%!!
Enjoy!

Ben

The most highly skilled Tree Ninja. For Ben, no job is impossible... it is just... well... interesting.

Martina

Martina is a fun-loving Ninja, who travels to work to enjoy the new things Ben tries to teach them all... she also cooks some amazing food!!

Jack

A very good worker filled with lots of sarcasm.
If there is something wrong, Jack will find it.

Kuba

Meet the most excited Ninja... Kuba! Always ready to go, with 100% energy! Kuba finds it very hard to relax...

Charley the Chipper

Charley's job is to eat the branches, and put the woodchip in a neat pile using his shoot on his back.

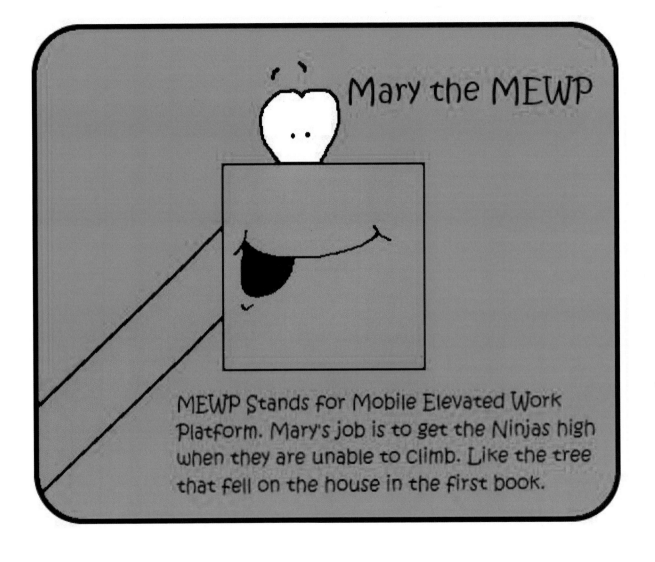

Mary the MEWP

MEWP stands for Mobile Elevated Work Platform. Mary's job is to get the Ninjas high when they are unable to climb. Like the tree that fell on the house in the first book.

Avi the Avant

Avi's job is to make sure the Tree Ninjas do not hurt themselves lifting up heavy logs. Avi has very strong teeth.

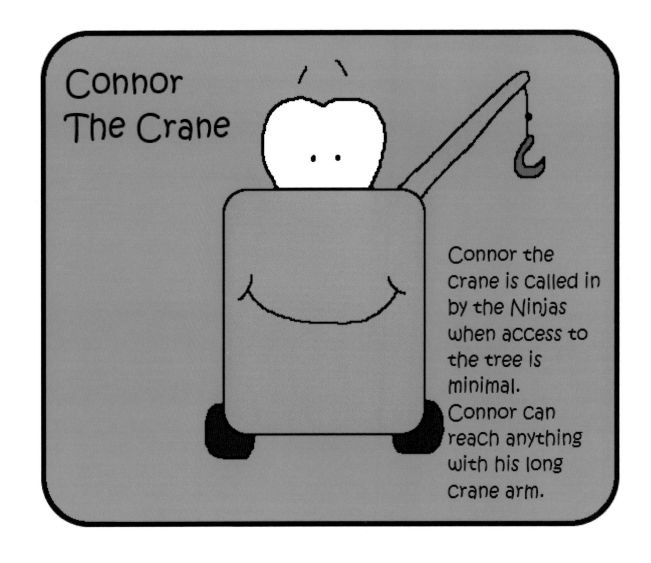

Connor The Crane

Connor the Crane is called in by the Ninjas when access to the tree is minimal. Connor can reach anything with his long crane arm.

Top handle Chainsaw

This chainsaw is used when the Ninjas need to climb, and cut a tree. It is very light, and easy to carry.

Chainsaw

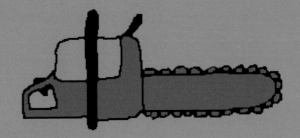

This is what the Tree Ninjas use to cut down, and prune trees.

TREE NINJAS

'The stick trick'

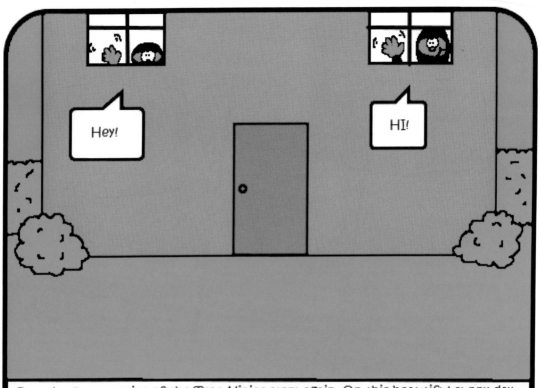

So... the great stories of the Tree Ninjas start again. On this beautiful sunny day, Ben, and Jack were already up and dressed ready for work. This was a very exciting day because Ben was going to teach Jack a very old trick used to measure where trees would fall... or was he??...

Oh yes! We can not forget Martina. Even she wanted to find out how amazing this would be!

Jack had never seen such a big, wide smile on Ben's face!

Both Jack, and Martina were very confused... surely it was too close to the house?? But they knew Ben had a plan... Ben always had a plan.

Ben had so much confidence in himself. He placed the stick exactly where the top of the tree would land.

Ben finished the directional felling cut. It was aimed perfectly towards the stick.

The customer took his phone out to make a video... but was he safe in his own house?

'Let's call Connor the Crane' said Ben in an excited voice.

Connor lowered Ben onto the top of the tree

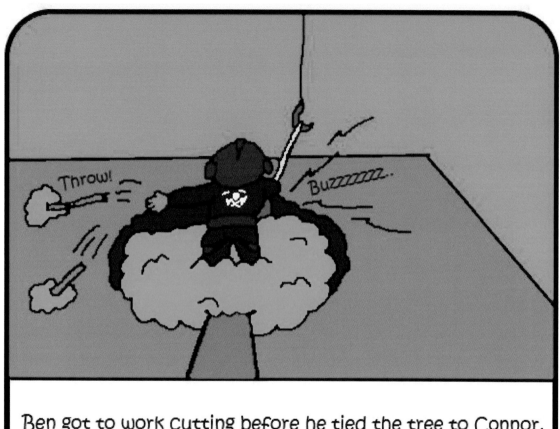

Ben got to work cutting before he tied the tree to Connor.

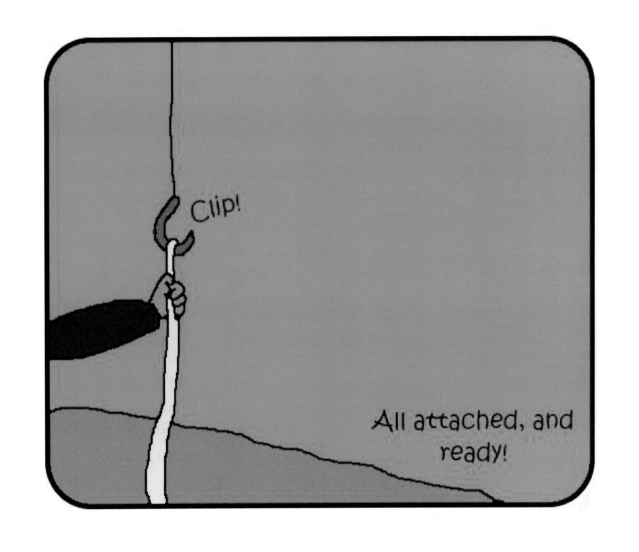

Ben got to the ground while Connor the crane waited for the signal to lift

Both Ben, and Connor were ready... but nobody asked the most important question...

Ben took one look at the Customer stuck in the tree, and decided the best option would be to move his legs... in the direction of home.

TREE NINJAS

'Bring your swimming costume'

Kuba was always the first Ninja awake. He was rarely ever seen, or heard. But everyday he was the reason Ben had food, and drink to last him all day.

Kuba was so lovely. He always liked to make Ben's life easy. So wherever possible Ben liked to return the favour. He thought to himself, 'Im going to do this job very quickly, and professionally, so that Kuba can have an easy day'...

'That is today's tree, Ben' said Kuba. 'The customer is worried about it falling in the water, so they would like to reduce it'... it just so happens it is down a steep bank, and has a very heavy lean! What a tough job for the Tree Ninjas...

When Ben stepped closer he realised that this would not be an easy job...

'Right' said Ben. 'Charlie you chip up the branches over there, and Kuba you get the rope. I have an idea!'

As Ben made his way up the heavy leaning tree, Kuba, Charlie the Chipper, and a lovely man fishing were watching in amazement.

What a great idea Ben had! He was going to drop the branches into the water, then Kuba was going to pull them out! Brilliant!!

One branch after another... the job could not go any better.

What an amazing team!!!

The branch fell the wrong way, and the rope went over the tree!! This was not good for Kuba...

The rope was not long enough, so Kuba held on for dear life!

The lovely man fishing started laughing, and could not stop!!!

And eventually...

So did Ben!

'Pull, Charlie!' howled Ben

Both Ben, and Charlie managed to get Kuba back on the grass, at the top of the hill. What great teamwork!

OH, NO! Kuba's hat was still in the water!

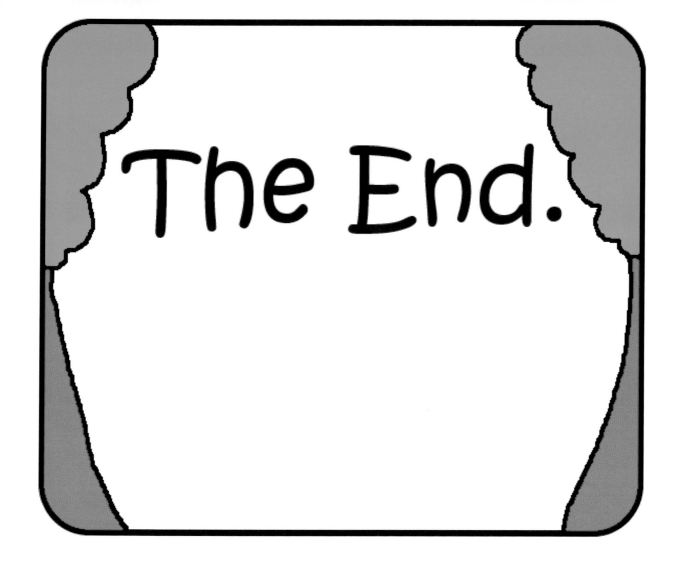

Chainsaw Woodcarving

15ft Giraffe carving in
Sawston, Cambridge.

Awesome bear carving in
March, Cambridgeshire.

Thankyou for reading our book!

You guys are awesome!

We hope to bring you
amazing stories again
soon...
Until the next time...

Tree Ninjas

100ft Lombardy Poplar...
with Ben in the top.

Printed in Great Britain
by Amazon

80828139R00036